THE SNOWSHOEING ADVENTURE OF MILTON DAUB,

BLIZZARD TREKKER

BY **MARGARET K. WETTERER** AND **CHARLES M. WETTERER**
ADAPTATION BY **EMMA CARLSON BERNE**
ILLLUSTRATED BY **ZACHARY TROVER**

Graphic Universe™ Minneapolis • New York

INTRODUCTION

FOR THREE DAYS IN MARCH 1888, A BLIZZARD RAGED THROUGHOUT THE NORTHEASTERN UNITED STATES. SNOW AND ICE BURIED THE LAND FROM MAINE TO MARYLAND. ROADS WERE CLOSED, AND HUNDREDS OF PASSENGER TRAINS WERE STUCK FOR DAYS BEHIND HUGE SNOWDRIFTS. WINDS, SOME OVER 80 MILES PER HOUR, CRACKED WINDOWS, TORE AWAY FENCES, ROOFS, AND SIGNS, AND TOPPLED TREES AND UTILITY POLES. THOUSANDS OF BIRDS FELL FROZEN FROM BUSHES AND BUILDINGS WHERE THEY HAD HUDDLED FOR SHELTER. MILES OF TELEPHONE AND TELEGRAPH WIRES SNAPPED UNDER THE PRESSURE OF WIND, ICE, AND SNOW.

CITIES, TOWNS, FARMS, AND FAMILIES WERE CUT OFF FROM ONE ANOTHER. FOR A TIME, THE GOVERNMENT IN WASHINGTON, D.C., LOST ALL CONTACT WITH THE REST OF THE COUNTRY. AT SEA, VIOLENT WINDS

AND WAVES DAMAGED COUNTLESS BOATS AND SANK MORE THAN TWO HUNDRED OF THEM.

MILTON DAUB WAS 12 YEARS OLD WHEN THE STORM STRUCK. HE AND HIS FAMILY LIVED IN THE BRONX, A TOWN THAT HAD BECOME PART OF NEW YORK CITY A FEW YEARS BEFORE. AT THE TIME, THE BRONX HAD A SMALL BUSINESS AND RESIDENTIAL CENTER WITH MILES OF FIELDS AND FARMS TO THE NORTH. THE DAUBS' TWO-STORY WOOD-FRAME HOUSE FACED 145TH STREET, A WIDE DIRT ROAD. MILTON WAS THE OLDEST OF FIVE CHILDREN. HE HAD TWO SISTERS, ELLA AND HANNAH, AND TWO BROTHERS, MAURICE AND JEROME.

THIS IS THE STORY OF MILTON DAUB'S ADVENTURE IN THAT TERRIBLE STORM, KNOWN EVER AFTER AS THE GREAT BLIZZARD OF '88.

5

AFTER BREAKFAST, MILTON AND HIS FATHER MADE SNOWSHOES OUT OF HEAVY CORD, WOODEN BARREL HOOPS, THIN SLATS, WIRE, AND THE SOLE OF AN OLD PAIR OF ROLLER SKATES.

HMM . . . DOES THIS LOOK LIKE THE PICTURE?

I THINK WE'VE GOT THE RIGHT IDEA, SON.

LET'S TRY THEM OUT!

WE'LL HAVE TO GO OUT AN UPSTAIRS WINDOW.

OKAY, MILTON, IF YOU START TO SINK, I'LL PULL YOU BACK.

WAIT, YOUNG MAN! CAN I BUY SOME OF THAT MILK?

WELL . . . SURE, I GUESS. IT'S TEN CENTS A CAN.

HERE'S A QUARTER. YOU DESERVE IT, WALKING AROUND IN THE STORM LIKE THAT.

I NEED MILK TOO.

ME TOO.

SOON, MILTON SOLD ALL OF HIS CANS OF MILK. HE SNOWSHOED BACK TO MR. ASH'S STORE AND BOUGHT MORE CONDENSED MILK.

BUT EVERY TIME HE PASSED A HOUSE, SOMEONE WOULD SHOUT FOR MILK. MILTON WENT BACK TO MR. ASH'S STORE A THIRD TIME.

I WISH I HAD A DOGSLED . . .

PUT ON YOUR NIGHTSHIRT AND GET IN BED, MILTON. I'M GOING TO BRING YOU SOME HOT SOUP.

MILTON ONLY ATE A LITTLE BIT OF THE SOUP. THEN HE FELL ASLEEP, EVEN THOUGH IT WAS ONLY SIX O'CLOCK.

THE SNOW FELL ALL DAY AND ALL NIGHT ON TUESDAY.

FINALLY, ON WEDNESDAY, THE STORM WAS OVER.

THE PEOPLE ALL TALKED ABOUT THE BOY WHO HAD WALKED ON SNOW THROUGH THE BLIZZARD TO HELP HIS NEIGHBORS.

MANY PEOPLE STOPPED BY TO THANK MILTON.

BUT ONE WOMAN COULD NOT THANK HIM ENOUGH.

MILTON, YOU HELPED SAVE MY HUSBAND'S LIFE.

I'M HAPPY I COULD HELP.

AFTERWORD

THE 1888 BLIZZARD SET RECORDS THAT HAVE NOT BEEN BROKEN EVEN AFTER MORE THAN A HUNDRED YEARS. THE NORTHEASTERN UNITED STATES HAS NEVER AGAIN SEEN SUCH A HUGE SNOWFALL OVER SUCH A LARGE AREA. WIND SPEED, SNOW LEVELS, AND LOW TEMPERATURE RECORDS FOR DOZENS OF PLACES IN THE AREA STILL STAND. BESIDES THE MANY PEOPLE WHO SUFFERED FROM FROSTBITE, EXHAUSTION, AND INJURIES FROM FALLS, MORE THAN 400 PEOPLE DIED DURING THE STORM. NEVER BEFORE OR SINCE HAS A BLIZZARD IN THE UNITED STATES TAKEN SO MANY LIVES. STORIES OF THE STORM BECAME PART OF AMERICAN FOLKLORE.

MILTON DAUB, HIS FAMILY, AND HIS NEIGHBORS NEVER FORGOT HIS SNOW WALKING DURING THE GREAT BLIZZARD OF '88.

FURTHER READING AND WEBSITES

BRONX CHRONOLOGY
HTTP://WWW.BRONXHISTORICALSOCIETY.ORG/BXHIST.HTML

BULLARD, LISA. *BLIZZARDS*. MINNEAPOLIS: LERNER PUBLICATIONS COMPANY, 2009.

FEMA FOR KIDS: WINTER STORMS
HTTP://WWW.FEMA.GOV/KIDS/WNTSTRM.HTM

FIGLEY, MARTY RHODES. *THE SCHOOLCHILDREN'S BLIZZARD*. MINNEAPOLIS: MILLBROOK PRESS, 2004.

HOW TO MAKE SNOWSHOES
HTTP://WWW.SURVIVALTOPICS.COM/SURVIVAL/HOW-TO-MAKE-SNOWSHOES/

MURPHY, JIM. *BLIZZARD! THE STORM THAT CHANGED AMERICA*. NEW YORK: SCHOLASTIC, 2000.

PBS KIDS: BIG APPLE HISTORY
HTTP://PBSKIDS.ORG/BIGAPPLEHISTORY/INDEX-FLASH.HTML

SNOW CRYSTALS WEBSITE
HTTP://WWW.ITS.CALTECH.EDU/~ATOMIC/SNOWCRYSTALS/

WADSWORTH, GINGER. *SURVIVAL IN THE SNOW*. MINNEAPOLIS: MILLBROOK PRESS, 2009.

A WALK THROUGH THE BRONX: INTERACTIVE MAP
HTTP://WWW.THIRTEEN.ORG/BRONX/MAP.HTML

WEB WEATHER FOR KIDS: BLIZZARDS AND WINTER WEATHER
HTTP://EO.UCAR.EDU/WEBWEATHER/BLIZZARDHOME.HTML

WHITELAW, IAN. *SNOW DOGS! RACERS OF THE NORTH*. NEW YORK: DORLING KINDERSLEY, 2008.

ABOUT THE AUTHORS

MARGARET K. WETTERER AND CHARLES M. WETTERER HAVE WRITTEN MANY BOOKS, INCLUDING SEVERAL CHILDREN'S BOOKS, FOR VARIOUS PUBLISHERS. THEY RESIDE IN HUNTINGTON, NEW YORK.

ABOUT THE ADAPTER

EMMA CARLSON BERNE HAS WRITTEN AND EDITED MORE THAN TWO DOZEN BOOKS FOR YOUNG PEOPLE, INCLUDING BIOGRAPHIES OF SUCH DIVERSE FIGURES AS CHRISTOPHER COLUMBUS, WILLIAM SHAKESPEARE, THE HILTON SISTERS, AND SNOOP DOGG. SHE HOLDS A MASTER'S DEGREE IN COMPOSITION AND RHETORIC FROM MIAMI UNIVERSITY. BERNE LIVES IN CINCINNATI, OHIO, WITH HER HUSBAND, AARON.

ABOUT THE ILLUSTRATOR

ZACHARY TROVER HAS BEEN DRAWING SINCE HE WAS OLD ENOUGH TO HOLD A PENCIL AND HASN'T STOPPED YET. YOU CAN FIND HIM LIVING SOMEWHERE IN THE MIDWEST WITH HIS EXTREMELY PATIENT WIFE AND TWO EXTREMELY IMPATIENT DOGS.

Text copyright © 2011 by Margaret K. Wetterer and Charles M. Wetterer
Illustrations © 2011 by Lerner Publishing Group, Inc.

Graphic Universe™ is a trademark of Lerner Publishing Group, Inc.

Graphic Universe™
A division of Lerner Publishing Group, Inc.
241 First Avenue North
Minneapolis, MN 55401 U.S.A.

Website address: www.lernerbooks.com

Library of Congress Cataloging-in-Publication Data

Wetterer, Margaret K.
      The snowshoeing adventure of Milton Daub, blizzard trekker / by Margaret K. and Charles M. Wetterer ; adapted by Emma Carlson Berne ; illustrator, Zachary Trover.
      p.   cm. — (History's kid heroes)
      Summary: An 1888 blizzard has paralyzed much of New England, but twelve-year-old Milton Daub puts on a pair of homemade snowshoes and braves the storm to bring food and medicine to many of his neighbors in the Bronx, New York.
      Includes bibliographical references.
      ISBN: 978-0-7613-6175-6 (lib. bdg/ : alk. paper)
      1. Daub, Milton—Juvenile fiction. 2. Blizzards—New York (State)—New York—History—19th century—Juvenile fiction. 3. Graphic novels. [1. Graphic novels. 2. Daub, Milton—Fiction. 3. Blizzards—Fiction. 4. Heroes—Fiction. 5. Adventure and adventurers—Fiction. 6. New York (N.Y.)—History—1865–1898—Fiction.] I. Wetterer, Charles M. II. Berne, Emma Carlson. III. Trover, Zachary, ill. IV. Title.
PZ7.7.W48Sno 2011
363.34'92509747275—dc22   2009051717

Manufactured in the United States of America
1—CG—7/15/10